SUICIDE CON

By

MATT FOX

ACKNOWLEDGEMENT

I want to express my sincere gratitude to faith and wisdom for providing me with the opportunity to write this book. For quite some time, I have aspired to break into the science fiction genre, and this project has finally allowed me to realize that long-held ambition.

As I began writing, I visualized the manuscript as a movie unfolding in my mind. This clear vision was instrumental in shaping and developing each chapter, guiding me through the entire writing process and providing continuous inspiration from beginning to end.

I extend my profound thanks to the entire team at Research Publishers for making this publication possible. With limited funding and a night job schedule, I found the quiet and focused time necessary to write and remain dedicated to my goal.

At 56 years old, I see this book as proof that it is never too late to create something meaningful. I intend to follow this story with a second book, **_Suicide Con 2_**, and will do my best to bring it to fruition.

Finally, I would like to extend my special thanks to Amy, my friend and liaison at Research Publishers, for her constant support and invaluable assistance throughout this journey.

DEDICATION

This manuscript is dedicated to a singular concept: that meaningful entertainment can flow from a good idea. I am grateful for the wisdom that guided me in bringing this concept to life.

I extend my sincere thanks to my team of editors. Their diligent work has been invaluable, rendering the manuscript more polished and enjoyable for the reader.

My family was unaware of this endeavor, as I chose to keep it private to avoid potential disappointment. Nevertheless, I am proud of my solitary efforts and my determination to craft entertaining books.

Finally, I extend my gratitude to every person who purchases this book. I hope that you find enjoyment within its pages.

TABLE OF CONTENTS

INTRODUCTION

What if the moment you chose to end your life was not an end, but a beginning? What if, at the very precipice of oblivion, you were offered a miraculous escape, unimaginable wealth, a second chance, and a purpose beyond your wildest dreams in exchange for welcoming a silent passenger into your mind? This is the compelling premise that launches The Host Accord, a genre-blending novel that explores the depths of human despair, the allure of redemption, and the profound consequences of choices made in our darkest hours.

Our story begins with **Rob Reid**, a man crushed by debt and despair, standing on the rain-slicked roof of a multi-storey car park. His decision is made; his life, he believes, is over. But destiny intervenes in the form of **Oma**, a small, sharply dressed man with an unsettling calm, who offers Rob an impossible deal: unimaginable wealth in exchange for becoming a *host*, a vessel for a symbiotic alien consciousness known as a **Lava**.

The Lavas are refugees from a distant, dying civilisation who use advanced time travel technology to find humans at the brink of death; those most open to their proposition. For them, it is survival. For Rob, it is escape. With nothing left to lose, he accepts.

. He awakens to a new life as a lottery winner, a homeowner in the picturesque town of Portrush, and a secret operative in an interstellar program he doesn't fully understand.

The Host Accord follows Rob as he is drawn deeper into Oma's world. He evolves from a beneficiary into an active agent, traveling through time to recruit other potential suicides, each mission a tense negotiation with death itself. He witnesses sporting history firsthand at the 1985 Mike Tyson fight and walks the hallowed grounds of St. Andrews during the 1984 Open. He experiences the breathtaking wonders of Beat-a, the Lavas' home planet, a utopia of constant daylight, AI-assisted living, and technological marvels where wants and needs are instantly met. Yet, this gilded cage comes with a price: the stress of the missions, the moral ambiguity of the work, and the gnawing loneliness for the messy, unpredictable reality of Earth.

The narrative escalates from a personal story of salvation into a gripping cosmic thriller when Rob discovers the true, staggering scale of the operation. Earth is not merely a recruitment ground; it is a storage facility in a vast, long-term demographic strategy. The ultimate goal is the mass relocation of all hosts to a newly constructed sister planet, a revelation that forces Rob to question whether he is a saviour or merely a pawn. His growing doubt leads to a final, desperate choice: to have his memories of Beat-a erased and return to his old life. Outwardly, he becomes an ordinary man again, yet somewhere deep within, a fragment of that other world remain

But the past, both personal and galactic, is not so easily escaped. The novel's final act explodes into a high-stakes conflict when the clandestine operations of Oma's people are discovered by the Temporal Transit Authority (T.T.A.), a shadowy organization dedicated to policing time travel. Rob is forcibly reawakened, his memories restored, and thrust into a dangerous cold war. The T.T.A. begins setting traps using fake suicides, aiming to capture the Lavas' technology. The balance of power shifts irrevocably when a time device falls into human hands, specifically a military faction with its own vision for humanity's future.

The Host Accord is more than a science fiction adventure. It is a layered exploration of sacrifice, identity, and the fragile fabric of reality. It asks whether the power to change the past is a curse or a cure, and whether two vastly different species, bound by circumstance and survival, can ever truly trust one another.

Through Rob's journey from a ledge of despair to the front lines of a temporal war, we are invited to explore the weight of memory, the meaning of home, and the unexpected alliances that can form when the survival of both worlds hangs in the balance. This is a story about the roads not taken, the lives saved in the nick of time, and the infinite ripples that echo from a single, desperate moment on a rainy night.

CHAPTER ONE
THE LEDGE

The rain fell in a fine, persistent mist, each droplet catching the jaundiced glow of the city's light pollution before splattering against the cold, gritty concrete. It was 11:03 PM on a Thursday, and a full moon hung like a spectral coin behind the veil of low-hanging clouds. Robert Reid stood on the top level of a multi-story car park, his hands gripping the rust-cool railing until his knuckles shone white.

The city below was a tapestry of moving lights and distant, muffled sounds, a world entirely divorced from the desolation that had taken root in his soul.

He was, by every metric he could calculate, ruined. Debts, like a nest of vipers, had coiled around his life, their constricting grip leaving no room for air or hope. The letters had stopped being threats and had become statements of fact: his failure was complete. There was no way back, no miraculous windfall, no last-minute reprieve. The sheer, vertical face of the car park offered the only clean escape from the chaos he had created.

His breath hitched, a sob catching in his throat. He fell to his knees, the wet asphalt soaking through his trousers. "Forgive me," he whispered, the words not a prayer but a plea into the uncaring void. His heart was a frantic drum against his ribs, a wild animal trapped in a cage of bone. He stood up, his body moving with a leaden heaviness that felt foreign. The rain chose that moment to cease, as if the universe itself was holding its breath. A car horn blared somewhere, absurdly normal. Life, oblivious, marched on.

He was limp, weary, a marionette with its strings cut. The final, terrible intention solidified in his mind, a cold and decisive crystal. He would step over. He would fly. He would be free.

A voice, clear and sharp, cut through the silence in his head. It was not his own.

"Wait!"

Robert froze, one hand still on the railing. Before him, the air itself seemed to fracture. It was not a sound but a sensation, a tearing of the fabric of reality. A shimmering rift, like a vertical tear in a painting, opened a few feet away. From this impossible aperture stepped a small man, no taller than Robert's chest. He was impeccably dressed in a simple, dark suit that seemed to absorb the light around it. His eyes were large and held a depth of intelligence that was immediately unsettling.

The man didn't waste a second. "If you had money," he snapped, his tone brisk and utterly devoid of emotion, "a significant quantity, would that halt your current course of action?"

Robert could only stare, his mind refusing to process the scene. Suicide was one thing; this was entirely another. He managed a numb nod.

"I can provide capital. A substantial amount," the man continued, his gaze unwavering. "In exchange, would you accept a symbiotic partnership? "A Lava requires a human host. Our planet is overpopulated, with more Lavas than available hosts. That is why we need hosts on Earth. Your world, particularly this region, has a regrettably high number of self-termination events. We use time travel technology to locate such moments and offer a mutually beneficial arrangement."

Robert found his voice, a hoarse croak. "A… Lava? Inside me? Is it painful?"

"The insertion is not painful. You swallow the vessel. The integration is seamless. You will remain, Robert Reid. Enhanced, perhaps. And wealthy beyond your current imaginings. This is a standard contract."

The surreality of the offer cut through his despair. It was insane. Impossible. Yet, the man stood there, solid and real, a fact that defied physics. The alternative was the void. What did he have to lose?

"I… I accept," Robert said, the words feeling both monumental and trivial.

The small man Oma gave a single, curt nod. He produced a small, smooth capsule that glowed with a soft, internal light. Robert took it and, with a final glance at the city he had been ready to leave, swallowed it. There was no taste, no sensation, just a quiet, settling warmth in his chest.

"The terms are concluded," Oma said. "Check your lottery ticket for last Saturday's draw, the triple rollover. You will find you hold the winning numbers. 7.5 million pounds should suffice for your debts and a new beginning. I will make contact in three months."

With that, Oma stepped back into the shimmering rift, which sealed behind him without a trace. Robert was alone again on the roof. The rain began to fall once more, but everything had changed.

Three months later, the debts were a memory. He had paid every last penny. He had bought a large, airy house with panoramic views of the sea in Portrush. He was Rob Reid, lottery winner. A man of fortune. And he was a host. The entity within him, which he had learned was named Lama, was a quiet, perceptive presence, like a passenger in the back seat of his mind. It had a fondness for the feeling of sunshine and, curiously, for the game of golf.

His old life had ended not on the asphalt, but in the signing of that silent contract. His new life was one of strange luxury and even stranger secrets.

CHAPTER TWO
THE GOLFER AND THE SUMMONS

The June morning was bright and clear over Portrush. At 9 AM precisely, Rob felt the familiar, soft pulse in his mind that signified an incoming communication. It was not a sound, but an impression, a knowing.

Oma calls tomorrow, the presence, Lama, communicated. A feeling of calm assurance accompanied the message. The Lava within him had grown accustomed to its home and had developed its own quirks. It enjoyed the meticulous nature of golf, the mathematics of wind and swing, the tranquility of the green expanse.

After a leisurely breakfast, Rob drove to the Portwart Golf Club. He had met two local men, Tom and Paddy, on the practice ground the previous week. Both were seasoned players, full of bluster and local knowledge, and had been amused by the wealthy newcomer who seemed to have luck on his side.

Their 11 AM tee time gave Rob plenty of opportunity to loosen up. He focused on his swing, feeling a unique sense of balance and clarity that he attributed to Lama's influence. His game had improved dramatically since the integration; his focus was laser-sharp, his hands steady.

Tom and Paddy arrived, their banter already in full flow. They spoke of great shots and past victories, their confidence bordering on arrogance. A friendly wager was proposed: five pounds for the winner.

The match was a quiet revelation for Rob. Where he had once been anxious and prone to error, he was now preternaturally calm. He played not to win, but to execute each shot with perfect form. He found the fairways, landed on the greens, and sank putts that made Tom shake his head in grudging admiration. Luck, it seemed, was indeed on his side, but it was a luck born of profound, unnatural focus.

He won the match and the modest wager. Tom, red-faced, clapped him on the back. "Incredible luck, son! That shot on the 16th? Had to be a one-in-a-million bounce!"

Rob smiled. "Just my day, I suppose."

He returned home, showered, and settled in for an early night. Oma's monthly visit was at 9 AM, and the encounters were often… eventful. He brewed a quick coffee the next morning, watching the clock tick down. At exactly 9 AM, there was no knock. Oma materialized in the center of Rob's living room, his usual composure shattered. He was agitated, wringing his small hands, his large eyes wide with alarm.

"What's wrong?" Rob asked, setting his coffee down.

"A host acquisition went critically wrong," Oma stated, his words rapid and clipped. "It has happened on rare occasions before. The subject attacked me."

"Attacked you? How?"

"The target is a high-value potential host named Michael," Oma explained. "He resides in East Belfast. He suffers from severe bipolar disorder. A Lava named Lori identifies him as a prime candidate. The neurochemical volatility of his condition, when combined with his medication, can be converted into a potent source of bio-energy. However, his instability also makes him unpredictable and dangerous. He is scheduled to fatally overdose tonight at 1 AM."

Oma paused, collecting himself.

"I moved in at 12:30 AM, counting on his medicated state to keep him calm. I miscalculated. Paranoia sharpened his every movement. He saw me as a threat, a hallucination made real. Then he lunged, fists and fury, and I had no choice but to pull back and retreat immediately."

Furthermore, he managed to call the police. Their response time is typically ten minutes, but they can arrive in five if a unit is nearby. The timeline is now compromised. I require your assistance."

Rob's mind, still struggling to grasp the reality of alien symbiotes and time travel, snagged on a point of terrifyingly mundane logic. "Hold on. How did you even know about him? How do you find these people... before it's too late? It's not like people advertise their lowest point."

Oma's large, penetrating eyes focused on Rob, and the agitation that had gripped him moments before seemed to solidify into a chilling, analytical calm. He smoothed his suit jacket with a precise flick of his hand. "A fundamental question. The process is less about clairvoyance and more about chronology. It is a systematic review of outcomes."

"Outcomes?" Rob asked, the words feeling cold and inappropriate.

"Indeed. In your world, death, especially a sudden or unattended one, is a formal affair. It generates paperwork. A discovery is made. Law enforcement is summoned. They create an initial report, a dry document that nonetheless contains the essential coordinates: a name, an address, a time of discovery, and an estimated time of death. A medical authority later confirms this. That official record, sitting in a digital database, is our point of entry."

Oma began a slow, measured pace across the living room carpet. "Our capabilities allow us to access these networks from a future point in the day, a week after the event." We are not predicting the future, Robert. We are reading the history of a tragedy that, from our operational vantage point, has already occurred. We then use our technology to travel back to a moment before that history was written. The time of death recorded in the report becomes our absolute deadline. We usually aim to arrive thirty to sixty minutes beforehand, a window we have found optimal for negotiation."

The horrific elegance of it dawned on Rob. They were auditors of fate, working backwards from a confirmed conclusion. "So, when you approach someone... You already have a report with their name on it? You know, for a fact, that they die?"

"In the timeline we intercept, yes. The event is a fixed point. Our intervention creates a new, divergent timeline where the report is never filed, and the individual becomes a beneficiary of the Host Accord. For example," Oma said, stopping his pacing to emphasize the point, "a report will be filed later tonight for a Michael John Green of 5 Entwistle Parade. "It will state that his body was discovered at approximately 1:15 AM, a presumed overdose. That document is our target. It gives us the location and the temporal coordinates. For Michael, we calculated that arriving at 12:30 AM offered the highest probability of a successful integration."

Rob tried to grapple with the scale of it. The idea that his own salvation had been just another line in a cosmic ledger was deeply unsettling. "But... there must be so many. How do you choose? You can't possibly get to everyone."

A faint, almost imperceptible tightening around Oma's eyes suggested this was a familiar and painful constraint. "That is the most significant limitation of our operation. Our resources, while advanced, are finite. We are forced to prioritize." He gestured vaguely, as if to the world outside. "Our analysts do not just look for deaths; they look for ideal candidates. They assess psychological profiles, biochemical compatibility with a Lava, and the potential for a clean integration. Some individuals, like Michael, possess a neurochemical volatility that is highly valuable once stabilized. They are considered 'high-yield' hosts. Others are selected for their resilience, or because their disappearance, should they choose to relocate, would create minimal investigative ripples. The Belfast region has a high concentration of viable candidates, but for every one we engage, many more are... logged and bypassed. The calculus is brutal but necessary."

The mission was no longer just about saving lives; it was a clinical, demographic operation. The lottery win and the new house weren't just gifts; they were payment for services rendered, based on his value as a viable host. The true drama was in this silent, invisible triage.

"The police," Rob said, his voice low. "The people who write those reports... they have no idea you're using them?"

"None whatsoever," Oma replied, his tone returning to its usual brisk efficiency. "From their perspective, it is a tragic case that will eventually be filed away. For us, it is a potential future secured. In this specific instance, that future is now unstable. The timeline is compromised, which is why I need your assistance."

Rob was stunned. "My assistance? What can I possibly do? If he attacked you, what chance do I have?"

"You are a success story, Robert," Oma said, his voice lowering. "You are living proof that the arrangement works. You are human. He may relate to you in a way that he saw me as a threat. You can explain the benefits. You can calm him. You can finish the negotiation that I could not."

CHAPTER THREE
THE INTERVENTION

Oma's plan was hastily constructed but precise.

"I believe you can manage this one," he said, pacing Rob's living room. "As a host, you can explain how we can help him. He is destitute. His electricity and gas are disconnected. His refrigerator is empty. His medication induces long periods of sleep, and he has lost all hope. This is the demographic we most frequently engage with."

Oma stopped and fixed Rob with a serious look "I must be candid. The previous attempt was not only unsuccessful—it compromised our anonymity. A surveillance team from the Temporal Transit Authority, the T.T.A., detected a trace of our operation on their monitors. The Authority exists solely to regulate and prevent unauthorized temporal movement, and although they have long suspected our presence, they have never been able to locate us. This incident, however, has sharpened their focus. We now have their full attention."

The revelation sent a chill down Rob's spine. His new life of luxury suddenly felt fragile, perched on the edge of a much larger and more dangerous world.

"We must proceed with caution," Oma continued. "I will send you back to 1 PM this past Thursday. He sleeps late due to his medication. The address is 5 Entwistle Parade, East Belfast. You are to take five hundred pounds in cash. Show him the money. Tell him there is infinitely more if he accepts. Inform him to expect a follow-up visit from me to formalize the contract."

Oma's expression grew graver. "For your protection, I am assigning two of my best operatives. They will escort you and remain cloaked nearby. Their sole purpose is to watch for T.T.A. agents. If they detect any presence, any at all, we abort immediately. You will be extracted. If the T.T.A. intervenes, the situation will become chaotic. The local authorities will likely attribute it to a violent psychotic episode on Michael's part. Do you understand the risks?"

Rob nodded, his mouth dry. "When do we leave?"

"In one hour."

The transition was, as always, profoundly disorienting. There was no sense of movement—only an abrupt and total replacement of reality. One moment he stood in his sunlit Portrush home; the next, he found himself on a cracked Belfast pavement beneath a slate-grey sky, two impassive escorts positioned at his sides.

They nodded toward a dilapidated terrace house.

As he approached the door, he felt a gentle nudge from within. It was Lama.

Be cautious, the Lava communicated. This one is fractured project calm.

Following an impulse, Rob folded the £500 and shoved it through the letter slot in the door. He heard a rustle from inside. A moment later, the door creaked open a few inches, revealing a sliver of a man's pale, tired face.

"What's this?" a voice rasped. "Who are you?"

"It's your lucky day," Rob said, keeping his voice low and even. "My name is Rob. I was in a situation very much like yours not long ago. Someone made me an offer that changed everything. The money is real. The opportunity is real. And that's just a fraction of what's available."

He told his story, omitting the more fantastic details, focusing on the despair and the miraculous financial rescue. He saw a flicker of hope in Michael's eyes, a light that had long been extinguished. The man was desperate, and desperation makes for a powerful persuader.

"There's a man named Oma," Rob finished. "He will come to you with the details, the contract. He is unusual, but he is legitimate. Just listen to what he has to say."

Michael looked from Rob's face to the cash in his hand. Finally, he gave a slow, hesitant nod. "Okay," he whispered. "Okay. I'll… I'll talk to him."

The agreement was made. Rob and his escorts slipped back down the street. As they reached the corner, two unmarked cars raced past them toward Michael's house. Rob's heart jumped into his throat. Was it the T.T.A.? The police?

His escort placed a hand on his arm. "It is nothing. Local social services. The timeline is secure."

They returned to the present, the mission accomplished. Michael had accepted.

CHAPTER FOUR
A TRICKY HOST AND A TRIP TO THE PAST

A week later, Oma visited Rob's home under less frantic circumstances. He accepted a cup of coffee, his demeanor once again calm and inscrutable.

"A satisfactory resolution," Oma stated. "It was a tricky host, but Michael has been successfully integrated. Lori is very content with the arrangement."

Rob felt a wave of relief.

"I'm glad to hear it." He finally voiced the question that had been troubling him. "Oma, not everyone I help can win the lottery. It would attract too much attention. So how is Michael's situation explained? How does a man with no money suddenly become wealthy?"

A rare, thin smile touched Oma's lips. "Ah. There are many avenues to sudden wealth. People win football bets all the time. Our time travel analysts provided Michael with the results of a complex twenty-match accumulator bet. Wins and draws, all predicted perfectly from his point in time. He placed a small, desperate bet, and it miraculously came through."

"How much?" Rob asked.

"Twenty thousand pounds. Enough to settle his immediate debts, restore his utilities, and grant him a fresh start. A modest sum, but life-changing for him. The bookmakers wrote it off as a poor outcome for them. No one questions it."

Oma seemed pleased. "The timeline has been corrected. The police were not involved. The outcome is positive for all parties."

With the crisis averted, life in Portrush resumed its peaceful rhythm. But a month later, during another scheduled visit on a rain-lashed Monday, Oma presented a new proposition.

"No golf today, Robert," Oma observed, watching the rain stream down the windows.

"No," Rob agreed. "A day for the indoors."

"You enjoy boxing, I believe?" Oma asked.

"I love it," Rob replied, curious.

"Several of our operatives are attending a historic boxing match. November 22nd, 1985. The event where a young Mike Tyson became the youngest heavyweight champion in history. It was a… cracker of a fight, as you might say. We have spare capacity on the transport. It would be a simple observational trip, a gesture of gratitude for your assistance last month. The time travel technicians will ensure we arrive at the correct moment and location. You will be perfectly safe."

The offer was incredible. To witness sporting history firsthand? It was an opportunity beyond any fan's wildest dreams. "I'd be honored to go," Rob said.

The transition to the past was, as before, instantaneous. One moment he was in his living room; the next he was hit by a wall of sound and heat. He stood in a vast, crowded arena, not far from the ring. The air was thick with cigarette smoke and the electric buzz of anticipation. The noise was deafening, a roaring and chanting beast of a crowd.

He was there. He could see the young, fearsome Mike Tyson and the champion, Trevor Berbick, in their corners. The bell rang. The fight was a brutal, short-lived masterpiece of power and aggression. Tyson's punches were not just seen but heard thudding, concussive impacts that echoed through the arena over the roar of the crowd. It was terrifying and magnificent.

The fight ended almost as soon as it began. Berbick was down, struggling to rise in a state of disorientation that spoke of a profound concussion. The crowd erupted. The new king had been crowned.

Rob returned home late that night, his ears still ringing, his mind buzzing with the visceral memory of what he had witnessed. It had been a flawless operation. A great night.

He went to bed feeling a unique connection to history, a secret witness to a legendary moment.

CHAPTER FIVE
THE RIPPLE

The fallout was not immediate. It arrived during Oma's next visit. He appeared in Rob's living room, but a stern, disapproving energy replaced the usual calm.

"The Tyson contest was indeed spectacular," Oma began, his tone sharp. "Mike would win again, many times. But a problem has arisen. A significant one."

Rob's sense of post-adventure euphoria evaporated. "What problem?"

"You left a ripple," Oma said coldly. "A trace of anachronistic energy. We were there, and the T.T.A. monitors are exceptionally sensitive to that kind of disturbance. They have had a field day with the data. And it gets worse. One of our team members, against all protocols, used a communication device to take a picture. A primitive Apple iPhone. The device's digital signature is a glaring anomaly in 1985. That image is now circulating on their internal networks.". It is, as you would say, 'all over their version of YouTube.' It has been there for years, from their temporal perspective."

Rob felt a cold knot form in his stomach. "Can't you go back and stop him? Fix it?"

"It is too risky," Oma replied flatly. "The T.T.A. will have already identified the exact event and time. They will have set temporal traps. Any attempt to correct the error would result in immediate interdiction and capture. They know of us anyway, but this has provided them with a specific, documented event to pursue."

"The individual responsible has been identified," Oma continued. "He has been suspended from all field operations for three months a lenient punishment, given the magnitude of his indiscretion. However, the primary consequence involves you. Their analysis of the footage revealed more than just the agent. They isolated you in the crowd, Robert. Your image is in their archives. I suggest you look it up."

Oma manipulated a small device. A holographic screen flickered to life in the air, displaying grainy, enhanced footage of the 1985 crowd. There, clear as day, was Rob's face, younger but unmistakably him, watching the fight with an expression of awe. He was a ghost in the machine of history, a man out of time.

A wave of cold dread washed over him. "Am I in trouble?"

"Not immediately," Oma said, deactivating the display. "But you are now a person of interest to them. If they ever manage to locate you in the present, you must say nothing. Do not engage, do not confirm, do not deny. You remain silent until I can arrange your extraction."

"Extraction? What's the worst-case scenario?"

"The worst-case outcome," Oma stated with chilling matter-of-factness, "is that you disappear."

"Where to?" Rob asked, his voice barely a whisper.

"To our home world. The T.T.A. will eventually catch up with us; it is an inevitability we have prepared for. We have hosts here on Earth, but we also maintain a thriving colony of humans on our own planet. It is a Class M world, perfectly suitable for your physiology. Many choose to emigrate because they find the complexities of Earth's society disagreeable. It is a one-way journey."

The final piece of a terrifying puzzle clicked into place in Rob's mind. "Is that… is that how so many people just vanish without a trace every year? People that no one ever finds?"

Oma met his gaze evenly. "Yes," he replied. "It is one of the methods."

"We are not conquerors, Robert. We are preservationists. Our planet is a sanctuary. You could visit it anytime you choose. Perhaps you should think about it."

With that, Oma departed, leaving Rob alone with a profound and terrifying new reality. The change in his life he had felt months ago was now a seismic shift. The fear of debt collectors was replaced by the existential terror of being identified by an agency that policed time itself. He was frightened in a way he had never been before.

Seeking normalcy, an anchor in the familiar, he decided it was time for some fried chicken from the KFC in Portrush. He took a long, unhurried drive along the coast road to Carnlough and back, the beauty of the landscape standing in stark contrast to the turmoil in his mind. That night he stepped into a long, hot shower, then went to bed early, letting the familiar strains of Classic FM wash over him as he tried to quiet the fear that now lingered in his home. His story was far from over.

CHAPTER SIX
A GLIMPSE OF ANOTHER WORLD

The revelation about the 1985 incident settled like a heavy fog over Rob's life in Portrush. He tried to immerse himself in the mundane to quiet his anxiety. He played golf, focusing on the mechanics of his swing, the feel of the grass under his feet, anything to distract from the fact that his image was now a data point in a temporal investigation. He shot a seventy-seven, with two birdies, a good score by any measure, but the victory felt hollow.

Two weeks later, Oma arrived for his monthly visit on a typically wet and miserable Northern Irish day. The usual briefing on operations was delivered with clinical efficiency.

"All is well," Oma began, sipping the tea Rob had offered. "There were eight potential host acquisitions last month, predominantly in the Belfast area. All struck a deal. However, two of them, upon integration, expressed a strong desire not to remain on Earth. They are fed up with it, to use their term. They have requested immediate relocation."

Oma placed his cup down precisely on its saucer. "I would like you to escort them to our home world."

Rob stuttered, his previous fears momentarily eclipsed by a surge of excitement. "Yes. Yes, of course. I'd love to."

He had fantasized about seeing Oma's origin planet since first learning of its existence.

The journey was set for the next morning at ten. The two hosts, Peter and Gillian, were quiet and seemed apprehensive yet resolute. They were accompanied by two of Oma's large, silent operatives, whose presence was more for logistical assurance than any perceived threat.

The process of transit was different this time. Instead of the instantaneous shift to a familiar location on Earth, there was a palpable sensation of movement, a prolonged moment of disorientation and pressure, as if moving through a dense medium. Then, it was over.

They stood in a stark, white corridor. Oma led them toward a set of imposing double doors. Light, bright, and constant, streamed through the seams. When the doors slid open without a sound, Rob was struck by a wave of sensations. The air was thin, yet warm and carrying unfamiliar scents, metallic, clean, and floral all at once.

The vista that unfolded before him was breathtaking. They were on a high balcony overlooking a city of impossible architecture. Skyscrapers of crystalline and polished metal soared into a salmon-colored sky, connected by graceful skyways. The air was filled with flying vehicles, drones, and sleek, silent taxis that moved in complex, yet orderly, patterns. The hum of activity was a constant, low thrum, the sound of a vastly advanced civilization.

"Drome technologies," Oma said, noting Rob's awe. "I believe your world is just beginning to discover the concept in 2025."

They were issued smooth, metallic key passes and credit cards máde from a strange, warm alloy. "You are our guests here," Oma said, his voice uncharacteristically gentle. "And you are well thought of. This drone taxi will take you to your quarters. The credit card is for any purchases you wish to make."

The shopping district was a marvel of automation. There were no staff. Large touchscreens allowed you to select items, such as shoes, clothing, and food. You specified size, color, style, tapped your card, and within minutes, your purchase would arrive at a collection point via a network of transparent tubes and chutes. The smell of food from one such terminal reminded Rob he was hungry. Chicken, he decided. Some things were universal.

CHAPTER SEVEN
THE CONSTANT DAY

Their accommodations were not just a room but a spacious, luxurious apartment, styled in a way that was both futuristic and comfortable, familiar yet alien. The most immediate and disconcerting feature was the light. It never changed. It was a perpetual, soft, midday glow.

Rob discovered the apartment's resident artificial intelligence, an entity named Troy that could communicate from any point in the room.

"Troy, when does it get dark here?" Rob asked.

The voice replied, calm and neutral, "Define dark."

"I mean, when do we lose the natural light? When does night fall?"

"We do not lose light. Light is constant. There is no night or day cycle in this sector. The illumination is regulated for optimal biological and psychological function."

No night. Daytime all the time. "Wow," Rob whispered to himself. It was profoundly different, and part of him found it unsettling, yet another part was fascinated. He could see how the comfort and ease of this place would make

Earth's struggles seem primitive and unappealing. The mystery of global missing persons cases had a compelling new explanation.

At what his internal clock told, him was noon, he asked Troy for food. "Do I have food in my apartment?"

"Yes, Rob. Chicken is ready in seven minutes. A red meat meal can be prepared in nine minutes. Would you like vegetables with your selection?"

"Chicken, please," Rob said.

It was ready in exactly seven minutes, cooked in a hydro-heater that preserved all its flavor and moisture. It tasted excellent. He washed it down with cranberry juice, which they had on hand, and finished with a serving of incredibly smooth, rich ice cream. Inside him, he felt a distinct pulse of contentment from Lama. The Lava was home.

Oma visited later. "How do you like it?" he asked.

"It's great," Rob said, still trying to process it all. "No night…"

"Is that a problem?" Oma inquired, watching him closely.

"No! No," Rob stammered quickly. "Not a problem. I like it. I really see now how so many people disappear from our world."

Oma explained further. The society featured vertical suites dedicated to entertainment, fully immersive reality simulations where one could book a time and place, from the 1940s to the 2050s, and a computer would construct a flawless world around them. There were golf courses too, including fantasy ones built with impossible geometries.

After Oma left to check on Peter and Gillian, Rob decided to explore. He asked Troy to acquire some gym gear for him, which he did with effortless efficiency through the apartment's delivery system. He then took the elevator to the fifth floor, which housed a gym, pool, and spa.

The facility was beyond anything on Earth. The equipment was sleek and responsive, adjusting to his physiology automatically. The instructors were AI holograms, offering perfect form correction and motivational support. Rob spent an hour marveling at it, a sanctuary of health and technology.

CHAPTER EIGHT
THE UNAVOIDABLE FUTURE

The start of Rob's second day on the alien world began with a breakfast prepared by Troy. He could easily grow accustomed to this life of effortless luxury. The apartment even had voice-controlled blackout blinds, allowing him to simulate night if he chose. His mind drifted to that night in the multi-story car park. If he had said no to Oma's proposal, he would never have experienced any of this. It was truly amazing. He now straddled two worlds: this futuristic, blessed wonderland, and Earth, where he had seven million pounds and a great, if complicated, life.

His reverie was interrupted by a knock at the door. It was one of the large, silent operatives Oma employed. "Rob. Time to go."

"Where are we going?" Rob asked. The man offered no reply, only stoic silence.

They entered a flying taxi and travelled for about ten minutes before landing at a stark and imposing government-style building. Inside, they found Oma waiting in a large circular chamber, seated alongside nine other individuals. Including him, there were ten in total. It was clearly some form of ruling panel or council.

A man in a sharp, two-tone red suit led the proceedings. He spoke with a calm, undeniable authority.

"Rob," he began, "I know this will seem strange, but our time travel analytics team has picked up a confirmed temporal anomaly. You were present in a group that was recorded using an Apple iPhone to take photographs at a sporting event in 1985. Is this correct?"

Rob looked at Oma, puzzled. "It wasn't me who took the picture. I would never"

"We know," the spokesman interrupted gently. "The individual responsible has been dealt with. However, the trouble is not the act itself, but its consequences in your personal timeline."

He manipulated a control, and a complex web of light, representing timelines, appeared in the air between them. "Our projections indicate that in 2026, next year from your Earthly perspective, you will offer a ride to a young female acquaintance. Unbeknownst to you, she will have a small quantity of cannabis. You will be pulled over by local law enforcement for a minor traffic violation, such as proceeding through a red light. The officer will smell the substance. You will both be arrested, photographed, and fingerprinted as standard procedure."

The light web zoomed in on a single node. "Here is the problem. Your arrest photo will be entered into a digital database. Facial recognition software, which will be ubiquitous by then, will run automatically. It will flag a one hundred per cent match with an individual in a crowd from 1985, someone who has not aged a single day in over forty years. This anomaly will be reported to the T.T.A. They will find you."

Rob's blood ran cold. "But I just won't pick her up! I'll avoid the situation entirely."

"The principle of the fixed point remains," the man replied. "The projection is not that you might be arrested. In the dominant timeline, you are arrested. Avoiding that specific girl or that specific light will not change the outcome. The variables will readjust another person, another infraction. The constant is that at some point in your life, you will be fingerprinted or formally photographed by an official Earth authority. Once that happens, the T.T.A. will be alerted. It is inevitable."

He let the gravity of the statement hang in the air. "It is too hard to go back to 1985 to fix the original error. The T.T.A. now constantly monitors that event. Any attempt would be immediately detected and could potentially uncover our entire operation. Your presence on Earth is now a permanent liability."

Rob could only manage a response. "I see." His mind raced. What now?

CHAPTER NINE
THE OFFER

The panel allowed Rob a moment to absorb the grim prognosis. The spokesman in the red suit continued, his tone shifting from explanatory to propositional.

"The council has a proposal for you, Robert Reid. You are welcome to stay here, on our world, as a permanent resident. You would be granted full citizenship, this apartment, and a generous stipend. In return, we would ask you to work with Oma. Your experience as a host and your success in recruiting others on Earth makes you a valuable asset. You would help us gain more hosts from your planet, guiding them through their transition as only someone who has lived it can."

Rob's thoughts immediately flew to his house in Portrush, his golf games, and the sea view. He loved his life there. But the council's offer was not really an offer; it was the only viable solution. If the T.T.A. captured him, their treatment of him was unlikely to be as generous or hospitable. He had no real choice.

"I understand," Rob said, his voice steady despite the turmoil within. "I accept your terms." Deep down, he knew it was true. He had grown fond of these people, of their quiet hospitality and calm composure. Even when delivering devastating news, they remained direct and never placed blame on him for what had happened.

The spokesman gave a firm, final nod. "Then it is settled. On Earth, you will become another missing person. Oma will be in touch with your first assignments. Good day."

The meeting was over. As Rob stood, feeling the weight of his decision, Oma approached him. "Welcome to a new beginning, Robert. You are a good man."

Rob managed a weak smile. "Not like I can argue about it."

Two days later, Oma arrived at the apartment with a data slate. "I have two potential host acquisitions this Saturday. We can manage both. Do you think you are ready?"

"Yes," Rob said, his resolve hardening. This was his life now.

"Both are prescription drug overdoses," Oma explained, pulling up the files. "The first is in Bangor, just outside Belfast. A bedsit. Small but manageable. Be very careful; the individual has a severe mental health condition. He is a prize host, and a Lava named Capri is very keen. The second is very close by. A homeless person on housing credit, living in a shelter on Southwell Road. We will approach at 11 PM with food a KFC bargain bucket. He will have no money and be hungry. The approach should be direct. We will offer five hundred pounds and the standard contract immediately. His

Lava is also very keen. Furthermore, I have secured a scratch card for him, worth one hundred thousand pounds."

Oma almost smiled. "Our operatives had to acquire three thousand scratch cards to find a winner. The logistics were somewhat amusing."

The missions were a success. The man in Bangor, though initially suspicious and unstable, was swayed by Rob's empathetic account of his own past despair and the immediate cash. The promise of a visit from Oma to finalize the contract sealed the deal. The homeless man on Southwell Road was easier; the offer of hot food and the life-changing scratch card was a miracle he could not refuse. His football bet story was already prepared.

"I can do this," Rob said to Oma after returning to the homeland.
"Good man," Oma replied. "You have a natural talent for it."

Exhausted, Rob went back to his apartment, where Troy had a warm dinner waiting for him.

CHAPTER TEN
A NEW NORMAL

The following morning, Oma met Rob for coffee. "This situation is good for you here, Robert. Your credit card will grant you access to almost anything you need within reason. Explore. Acclimatize."

"Can I go shopping, then?" Rob asked, feeling a need for normalcy.

"Yes," Oma said. "Knock yourself out."

Rob turned to the apartment's AI. "Troy, can you call a taxi to take me to the stores?"

"You can order anything you require online, Rob," Troy's voice replied. "Goods from the Ventural District can be delivered directly to the apartment."

"I know, Troy, but I'd like to see the town. Can I shop in the physical stores?"

"Yes," Troy answered. "However, it is not the most common method of procurement. I will book a taxi for you."

It was Rob's first trip alone in a flying taxi. The vehicle was sleek and cool, arriving silently at his balcony. The journey was swift and smooth, offering breathtaking aerial views of the city before landing at a vast commercial plaza.

The stores were vast and echoingly quiet. Upon entering, he found the setup was similar to the automated systems he'd seen before, just on a grander scale. Giant television screens displayed products, and when he made a selection this time gym wear and tapped his card, the items shot down from a complex network of overhead tubes. He ordered five items and waited less than three minutes for them to be bagged and presented to him. The efficiency was astounding.

After shopping, he felt hungry. His Lava, Lama, communicated a strong desire for KFC. He found a food terminal and discovered a local variant called "Funky Chicken," seasoned with a garlic salt that was new to him but utterly delicious. He felt a wave of gratitude from the Lama.

He was amazed by the people. They were well-mannered and appeared content, though they engaged in very little casual chatter. He noticed that if he mentioned a neutral topic, such as the weather or the climate, they would happily chirp up and engage. He found himself missing the noisy, chaotic charm of regular cars, wondering if this drone technology would ever be introduced on Earth, and if so, how humanity would adapt.

The taxi ranks were unmanned. He pressed a button, gave his voice address "Cobel Apartments," and a vehicle glided over. He got in, and two safety bars gently curved over his chest, reminiscent of the restraints on bumper cars back in Portrush. The taxi lifted straight up and flew, depositing him at his apartment building in just three minutes.

Troy was there, the apartment spotless. "Happy shopping, Rob?"

"Yes, Troy, thank you. Could I have some cranberry juice, please?"

He sat down in his new dwelling, his purchases in hand, as a glass of juice materialised on the side table, delivered by a small domestic drone. He looked around, still uncertain whether any of it felt truly real. But it was. This was his life now.

He asked Troy for some classical music.

"Define classical," Troy requested.

"Instrumental music from the eighteenth and nineteenth centuries on Earth. Orchestral."

"Definition accepted. Playing selection."

The room was filled with the soft, familiar strains of a symphony. It was nice music. For the first time since his arrival, surrounded by the comforts of this advanced world and the echoes of his own, Rob felt a sense of peace. He leaned back, closed his eyes, and fell asleep.

CHAPTER ELEVEN
THE PERKS AND PRESSURES OF THE JOB

A week after his relocation became permanent; Rob was summoned to a briefing with the same panel that had interviewed him. He arrived at the severe government building at 11 AM sharp. The atmosphere was less confrontational this time, though the formality remained.

"Please, have a seat, Robert," the spokesman in the red suit said. Rob sat. "The mission you undertook last week, escorting the hosts Peter and Gillian, was executed flawlessly. Your transition into your new role is proceeding well. Do you find your new posting agreeable?"

"It is fine," Rob replied, choosing his words carefully. "It is an adjustment, but I am adapting."

"Good. You will not be required to work every week. While tragic, the frequency of suitable host acquisitions does not demand constant intervention. Our temporal analysts have looked ahead. There are no projected suicides in your designated area for the next two weeks. However, there is a predicted event after that period which is expected to be particularly challenging."

The spokesman manipulated a holographic display, bringing up a file. "A marital breakdown. A broken heart. These cases are always the most difficult, as they are not motivated by financial desperation. The subject is a woman residing in a large property on Warren Road in Donaghadee. She will discover that her husband has been unfaithful on multiple occasions. They are wealthy. Therefore, our usual bargaining chip financial salvation is irrelevant. You must be prepared for a refusal. We lose many of these types. Our only offer can be a new beginning here on Beat-a, or if she is single, the possibility of a partner match through our systems. The primary objective is to secure the host for the Lava."

The man looked at Rob directly. "I do not want you to believe this role is solely comprised of easy victories. These emotional cases require a delicate touch you are still developing."

Seeking to lighten the mood or to test Rob's integration, the spokesman changed the subject. "You have two weeks of leave. Is there somewhere you would like to go? Somewhere in the past, perhaps?"

The question stunned Rob. The possibilities were infinite. Then, a thought crystallized. Seve Ballesteros. The 1984 Open Championship at St. Andrews. Could I attend?"

The spokesman nodded. "That can be arranged. Consider it a perk of the job. The usual protocols apply: stay away from cameras and avoid any interaction that could leave a trace. Oma will prepare the necessary arrangements for the trip. When would you like to go?"

"Just the final day. Sunday. A seat in the grandstand would be perfect."

"Very well. We will send you on the Saturday. You can stay at a vacant room at the University of St. Andrews; it is closed for the holidays. Our operatives will provide you with period appropriate clothing and currency for the time. One of our operatives, Tam, will travel with you. When would you like to depart?"

"Tomorrow, if possible," Rob said, his excitement growing.

"Give us the time to set it up. You will leave tomorrow."

The next morning, after a full breakfast prepared by Troy, Tam met him at the apartment. The transit was seamless. They did not need to stay the night, but the connection point was established there. The following day, Rob found himself sitting in the grandstand overlooking the 18th hole of the Old Course. The historic atmosphere was electric. He spent the entire day watching the drama unfold, culminating in Seve Ballesteros holing the winning putt on the final green, triumphing over Tom Watson. It was a perfect, immersive piece of history, and Rob felt a profound gratitude for the strange turn his life had taken.

CHAPTER TWELVE
THE COMPLEXITIES OF A NEW SOCIETY

Rob returned from 1984 without any complications. The familiar environment of his apartment on Beat-a was a welcome contrast to the windy Scottish links. Troy, as always, was waiting.

"Did you have a successful trip, Rob? Would you like a cranberry juice?" the AI inquired.

"Yes, Troy, thank you," Rob said, taking the glass that materialised. "It really is great having an AI like you. You are incredibly helpful."

Having Troy as a constant resource had made his acclimatisation far smoother. He found himself asking endless questions about his new home, a Class M planet he had learned was officially named Beat-a. The more he discovered, the more fascinated he became, though he still held a soft spot for simple pleasures like the local "Funky Chicken," which was, in his opinion, a far superior version of Earth's KFC.

His mind, however, was already turning to his next assignment: the difficult host acquisition in Donaghadee. He knew the area well from his life on Earth. His strategy would have to be different. He would need to make the concept of Beat-a sound like a sanctuary, not just an escape. The offer of a partner matching service, like an advanced dating agency, might be a key incentive.

Through his conversations with Oma and Troy, Rob was learning more about the complex social structure of his new home. Most human residents on Beat-a were hosts to Lavas. Oma had explained that hosts could lead normal lives, but the rules of procreation were different and critical to the Lavas' survival. If a host couple had a child, a female baby would become a "Queen," not royalty in a political sense, but a biological producer of Lavas. This was why the lava population was so high. Hosts were limited to one child to control population growth, and the Lavas considered themselves fortunate that not every birth resulted in a female, which would place a great biological responsibility on the child.

Curiosity mixed with a deep sense of unease, compelled Rob to finally ask the question that had been forming in his mind.
"Oma… you call them 'Queens'. But what are the Lavas, exactly? Where do they come from? And if they're not the children, how are they created?"

Oma regarded him with a thoughtful silence, as if deciding how much of the foundational truth to reveal. "The Lavas," he began, his voice taking on a rare, almost reverent tone, "are the original consciousness of this world. Our physical forms, the ones you see, are merely vessels biological suits designed for interaction and survival. Our true essence is non-corporeal. We are energy. Thought. A collective mind that, over millennia, faced a slow dissipation, a fading from existence."

He gestured to the cityscape beyond the window. "This civilization, all that you see, was built as a life-support system. A magnificent cage to preserve a dying race. We developed the technology to travel not through space, but through time, seeking a solution. We discovered that the human brain, with its unique complexity and emotional resonance, could act as a perfect stabilizer and amplifier for our consciousness. A symbiotic host provides the necessary biological anchor we lack."

"So, the Lava inside me... Lama... it's like a refugee?" Rob asked, the concept making the presence in his mind feel suddenly more vulnerable.

"A refugee. A passenger. A partner. All are correct," Oma acknowledged. "But for our species to have a future beyond mere preservation, we needed a way to reproduce. To create new Lavas. This is where the 'Queens' become essential." He leaned forward, his large eyes intent. "The union of two hosts creates a unique biochemical environment. When a female child is conceived and born under the influence of two symbiotes, her biology undergoes a subtle but profound change. She becomes a nexus. Upon reaching maturity, her own endocrine and neurological systems do not simply sustain a Lava; they have the capacity to generate new ones. It is a natural, cellular process. She doesn't choose it; she is it. A single Queen can, over her lifetime, produce thousands of new Lavas, each a unique consciousness."

"The ultimate renewable resource," Rob murmured the scale of it staggering.

"Precisely. That is why population control is not merely a social policy; it is a matter of galactic-scale responsibility. An unchecked number of Queens would lead to an impossible population explosion. Conversely, too few would mean our species stagnates. It is a delicate balance. And it is also why the Lavas are so beneficial to their hosts. The symbiosis is not one-sided."

"In what way?" Rob pressed, thinking of his own improved golf game and sense of calm.

"The presence of a Lava has a harmonizing effect on the human body," Oma explained. "It boosts the immune system significantly hosts rarely suffer from terrestrial illnesses. It enhances physical strength and neural coordination, as you have experienced. But perhaps most importantly, it can repair and stabilize mental health issues. The Lava's consciousness acts as a regulator, smoothing out the neurochemical imbalances that lead to depression, anxiety, and the very despair that made you, and others, ideal candidates. It is a fair trade: we gain an anchor to life, and you gain a healthier, enhanced one."

The explanation settled over Rob. The entire operation, from the desperate interventions on rainy rooftops to the sprawling cities on Beat-a, was part of an intricate, generations-long survival strategy. He was not merely a man who had won the lottery; he was a vital cell within a living, breathing organism fighting for its future.

The Lavas weren't invaders; they were desperate survivors, and their salvation was intrinsically tied to humanity's own brokenness.

This was just another complex layer to a situation Rob already found challenging. He was determined to succeed, hoping a victory would please the panel and solidify his position.

In his downtime, he made use of the communal gym in his apartment complex. His strength had improved noticeably, a change he credited to Lama's influence. The Lava seemed to thrive on physical exertion, and he suspected some of that energy had rubbed off on him. He also began to notice other residents, including several attractive women. They all knew he was new, and they knew who he worked for, but he had not yet summoned the courage to start a conversation.

Despite the comforts, pangs of nostalgia hit him. He missed his golf clubs, his house in Portrush, and the simple act of driving his car. Oma had updated him: a missing person report had been filed for Robert Reid. His house was under police investigation, but nothing suspicious had been found. The official story would eventually blow over, and another life would be quietly closed.

The mission to recruit women in Donaghadee proceeded. Traveling back to the precise moment of her despair, Rob found her terrified and broken. He gently explained his own host experience, how he was acquired, and vividly described the wonders of Beat-a. He emphasized the support systems, including the partner matching service. After a long, emotional conversation, she agreed. She left for Beat-a, and a clean-up team was dispatched to ensure no evidence of the intervention remained. It was a hard-fought success.

CHAPTER THIRTEEN
A NEW HOME AND AN AMERICAN DREAM

Rob accompanied the new host, a woman named Claire, to Beat-a. Her disorientation was palpable. "Where is this place?" she whispered, looking around the arrival terminal.

"It is called Beat-a. It is in a different galaxy, far from Earth," Rob explained gently, handing her a credit card. "This will allow you to purchase anything you need: food, clothes, anything."

In her new apartment, a personal AI unit named Trish greeted her. "Claire, would you like food, coffee, or tea?" Trish asked.

"Yes, could I have a peppermint tea, please?" Claire replied, her voice still shaky.

"Yes, of course," Trish said.

Rob showed her around the spacious apartment, pointing out the well-stocked wardrobe, which included a comfortable dressing gown. "Trish will instruct you on how to use the shopping systems tomorrow. The clothes here are great," he assured her before taking his leave.

Returning to his own apartment, Rob felt a sense of accomplishment. The operations team was pleased. Troy poured him a cranberry juice, and he retired to bed, exhausted but satisfied.

The next morning, Tam knocked on his door. "Briefing, Rob. Ten minutes," he said in his characteristically quiet voice.

He was brought before the same ten-member panel. Oma spoke highly of his handling of the Claire situation, noting his empathy and persuasion skills. The spokesman agreed. "We normally have to cut loose from hosts who refuse the program in such emotional cases. Your success rate is notable." They asked about Tam's performance as his operative, and Rob gave a positive report.

The briefing expanded his understanding of the operation. "This process is ongoing all across the globe on Earth," the spokesman explained. "We have different teams allocated for different regions. America, for instance, has a high volume of suicides. A very large crew is dedicated to covering that territory."

"Now, back to your area," the man continued. "There are no more projected events until next Friday. You have a few days off." He paused. "Do you miss your golf?"

"Yes, I do," Rob admitted.

"Would you like to play in America?"

The question surprised him. "Yes, I would."

"Our operatives who collect hosts in the United States will give you a game. Oma can introduce you to them. It can be arranged."

"Thank you," Rob said, genuinely touched by the gesture. The withdrawal from golf had been real for him. True to their word, Oma arranged a trip. Rob found himself playing a round at the legendary Pebble Beach Golf Links. It was just for a day, but it was magnificent. There were no complications. He hired clubs and played with Tam and another operative named Reunie. The weather was perfect, hot with a clear blue sky. They gave him easy assignments to observe, a light workload for such a reward. Returning to Beat-a that evening, he realized with a start that he was now referring to it as "back home." The connection was deepening.

CHAPTER FOURTEEN
A DANGEROUS FAILURE

Life on Beat-a was becoming his new normal. It was an exciting place. Claire had settled in well, her life improving dramatically. She loved the shopping opportunities and the sheer variety of goods available. Rob fell into a routine: gym at 7 AM, followed by breakfast.

One morning, as he was considering trying the virtual reality suite for the first time, Tam knocked on his door. "Don't head out, Rob. Oma has a job for you. But first, you are getting chipped today."

"Chipped? What is that?" Rob asked.

"It is a safety precaution," Tam explained. "A small neural tracker. If a job goes badly, you can activate a panic button mentally. It will allow us to extract you immediately. It is designed to prevent attacks. You will soon begin undertaking some solo missions."

Oma arrived shortly after, and they left for a medical lab via drone taxi. The procedure was quick. Rob was given a mild sedative, a small injection administered directly into his neural pathway, which required sedation for precision. Lama conveyed a sense of confusion and discomfort, as the Lava did not appreciate the chemical interference in their shared system. Afterwards, Rob was given a cup of tea and some shortbread to help stabilise his blood sugar.

It was only then that Oma briefed him on the new assignment. "This one is not going to be easy, Robert. The subject is on prescription medication for severe psychological issues. He has profound misanthropy; he does not like people. The event occurred last night. He died by a self-inflicted gunshot wound."

Rob stared at him. "He has a gun?"

"Yes," Oma said flatly. "That is why the chip was installed today."

Oma detailed the man's situation. "He was a long haul lorry driver, making good money crossing borders. He invested in properties to rent, becoming a private landlord. Then the housing market crashed. He is now in negative equity on three properties he owns. To make it worse, a tenant is refusing to pay rent. He works long hours and is simply tired of everything. He died at 3 AM, and he had been drinking. The gun was loaded and within reach."

Oma's plan was risky. "I will send you back to 1 AM. Take a bag of Chinese food as a pretext to gain entry. Once inside, explain the contract and the money. We want this host badly. Our superiors say we are behind quota for the Belfast area. He would be a good host, but he is a difficult acquisition."

Rob was sent back. He arrived at 1 AM, holding the bag of food. The man, Brian, answered the door and immediately became hostile. "I didn't order any food!" he snarled.

"Can I come in and explain?" Rob asked, trying to sound calm.

"No!" the man yelled, trying to slam the door.

In a split-second decision, Rob pushed his way inside. The man's eyes widened in rage and paranoia. He lunged toward a side table where the gun lay. Rob didn't hesitate. He hit the mental panic button.

There was a violent lurch, a sensation of being ripped backwards through a tunnel. A moment later, he was staggering in the lab on Beat-a, the smell of Chinese food still clinging to his clothes. The mission was a failure. His first one. The reality of the danger he was in settled heavily upon him. This was a hard, and sometimes impossible, job.

CHAPTER FIFTEEN
A SISTER WORLD AND A DAY AT THE LAKES

Oma was waiting for him in the lab. "The job could not be done. That man, Brian, was impossible. I am sorry you had to experience that."

"It is alright," Rob said, his heart still racing. "It was far too hostile. I see that now."

"I know," Oma replied. "We were aware it was a very high-risk assignment. That is precisely why we fitted the panic button and the neural chip first. Do not worry, Robert. It was worth an attempt. These things happen."

Shaken, Rob asked for a few days off. Oma agreed immediately.

Returning to his apartment, Rob was greeted by the fresh, clean scent of cotton. Troy had been cleaning. The AI, sensing his need for distraction, suggested an outing. "You have a few days off. Would you like a tour? You have not seen much of our world beyond the city."

Troy ordered a taxi. "Where are we going?" Rob asked.

"The Lakes of Oran. They are approximately thirty minutes from the city. Mountains, fresh water, and a restaurant that is said to serve excellent food."

The trip was a balm for his nerves. The lakes were stunningly beautiful, set against a backdrop of purple mountains. The restaurant, built on a pier over the water, did indeed serve excellent food, including a chicken dish that Lama approved of heartily.

As they enjoyed the view, Troy provided more information about Beat-a's expansion. "Did you know that Beat-a has a sister planet? It is not as built up in its development. Beat-a is running out of space, and we are now placing hosts on this new world. Construction bots are working tirelessly; they are remarkably quick to erect buildings. It has been under development for two years now."

Rob was intrigued. "What is it like?"

"It has far more open land dedicated to recreation. Golf courses, athletic tracks, tennis complexes, equestrian centres, and motor racing circuits. It is intended for pleasure trips, as so much of Beat-a's land is now used for housing. Would you like to see it someday?"

"Could I?"

"Yes, it is not a secret. People are already visiting as some sections are finished. The car racing track is complete a large professional circuit with two smaller tracks for beginners. The cars are similar to your luxury high performance vehicles on Earth. Hosts can book trips there. It will be populated soon. Some cities are finished, though initially, only the highest-ranking individuals on Beat-a are allowed to relocate there. Given your position in operations, you would likely qualify. It is less crowded there."

They spent the rest of the day at the lakes, watching boats cruise on the clear water and children playing on paddleboards. Rob noticed a demographic oddity. "There are lots of boys here," he observed.

"Yes," Troy replied. "I agree. Female children are statistically limited. As you know, if two hosts have a child, a boy introduces no change to the population. But a baby girl becomes a Queen, a producer of Lavas. This is why we have an abundance of Lavas in need of hosts."

The day provided a much-needed respite, offering Rob a glimpse of the quieter, recreational side of his new existence and hinting at a future of even greater expansion and possibility.

CHAPTER SIXTEEN
REVELATIONS AND A PLANNED ESCAPE

The day spent at the Lakes of Oran was a temporary respite, but the stunning vistas could not completely quiet the turmoil in Rob's mind. The concept of the sister planet, Beta-a 2, was appealing. A smaller population, expansive golf courses, and open spaces sounded like a paradise compared to the increasingly regulated and crowded life on Beat-a. The idea of visiting it filled him with a keen sense of anticipation.

Upon returning to his apartment, he made his way down to the "Funky Chicken" outlet, finding comfort in the familiar taste. Lama also expressed his appreciation for the meal, a rare point of uncomplicated agreement between host and Lava.

Back in the quiet of his apartment, Rob turned to Troy.

"Troy, could I go to the sister planet tomorrow? I am very keen to see it."

The AI was silent for three seconds, a sign it was accessing and processing far-flung data streams. "A shuttle departs at 1 PM tomorrow. Its primary function is to deliver construction bots like myself to speed up the work on C Block, a massive residential structure designed to house thirty thousand individuals. Hosts with specific credentials will merit occupation. However, there is passenger capacity available."

Then, Troy offered information Rob had not solicited. "Rob, were you informed about the long term plan for the hosts on Earth?"

"No. What plan?"

"The strategic objective is to eventually transplant them. All of them. From Earth to the sister planet."

Rob was stunned. "All of them? But there are thousands of hosts on Earth."

"Yes. The administration believes the new planet will be a significant success, a place of pure perfection. They are waiting until the infrastructure on Beta-a 2 is more developed. Construction is proceeding at an accelerated pace due to the constant light; the bots can work twenty four hours a day without interruption."

The scale of the plan was a shock.

"The hope is that this will alleviate the population pressure on Beat-a," Troy continued. "As you know, with such a large population, everyone is not allowed out at once. Your designated times for civic movement, from 1 PM to 4 PM and 7 PM to 9 PM, are rationed to prevent logjams and system overloads. This is why work on the sister planet is proceeding at maximum capacity."

Then came the most devastating piece of truth. "We used Earth as a storage facility for Lavas. The plan was always to bring them home, along with their hosts, eventually."

The realization hit Rob like a physical blow. "No way. I did not know this." A cold feeling settled in his stomach. "Troy, are you telling me I am being used? That we all are?"

The AI's response was neutral, yet it felt like an apology. "Rob, I am sorry, but that is the functional reality of the program. You are a component in a larger demographic strategy."

Rob's mind raced. "Yeah, but... I did agree to it. I was about to die. They saved me."

"Do you like it here?" Troy asked.

The question was simple, but the answer was complex. "Yes... well, that is ok then," Rob replied, though his conviction was gone. "Would you like tea?" he asked, deflecting.

"I think I will have an early night," he said instead. "Can you put some classical music on?"

"Yes, indeed," Troy replied, and the room filled with soft, soothing strings. But Rob could not be soothed. The illusion had been shattered. He was a prisoner in a gilded cage, a pawn in a game whose rules he had never fully understood.

CHAPTER SEVENTEEN
A GLIMPSE OF THE FUTURE

Despite his misgivings, Rob could not suppress his curiosity about Beta-a 2. He had a good time at the lakes, but he couldn't stop thinking about the implications of hosts being pulled from Earth.

If there were over three thousand in Northern Ireland alone, the number across America must be vast, perhaps a hundred thousand. The scale of the operation was staggering. They were being used as temporary storage to be relocated later. It was a brilliant, if morally ambiguous, strategy, as long as the hosts ultimately agreed.

Troy had prepared him some food for the trip, warning that amenities on the sister planet were still scarce. The transport shuttle was utilitarian, a type of cargo ship filled with tools, construction materials, and silent, identical bots. There was just enough room for passengers.

The journey took half an hour. The arrival on Beta-a 2 was dramatic. Even before the doors opened, he could hear the high-pitched whine of powerful engines winding around a track and smell the faint, acrid scent of burnt fuel. As he stepped out, Troy gestured toward the source of the noise. "That section is finished. A large stadium and dedicated racing vehicles."

The vista was one of controlled chaos. He could see half-finished cities being constructed at an incredible pace by swarms of bots. The landscape was intentionally flat and sculpted, with a massive park already taking shape in the middle of the construction zone. It was a wonderful, raw display of power and planning.

"It is approximately one year from being ready for its first phase of occupation," Troy stated.

"I am glad I had breakfast," Rob remarked, seeing nowhere to purchase food.

"We have two hours before the transport returns," Troy said. "If we miss it, the next one is in five hours."

"There is a finished golf resort. I would like to see that."

"It will be empty, but if we have time, we can go."

They took a flying car to the resort. It was a magnificent place, with vast, powder white sand bunkers and water features integrated throughout the course. There were multiple tee boxes for different skill levels, all meticulously maintained and very tidy. It was a golfer's dream, but its emptiness gave it a ghostly, unreal quality.

They made their way back to the transport with time to spare. The shuttle returned them to Beat-a. Troy prepared a salad for him upon their return. He had just finished eating when Tam knocked on his door.

"Oma wants to see you in the morning," Tam said quietly.

"Okay," Rob replied.

The next morning, Oma arrived for coffee. He seemed his usual efficient self. "Two acquisitions on Saturday. They should be easy ones. Both are money related. Easy peasy."

Oma began to fill him in on the details, but Rob was only half listening. His mind was on the vast, empty golf course and the silent, rising cities on Beta-a 2, a future being built on a foundation of hidden truths.

CHAPTER EIGHTEEN
THE CHOICE FOR NORMALCY

The briefing with Oma was the final straw. The stress of the jobs, the intrusive nature of the constant technology, and the crushing revelation from Troy about his role in a grand demographic scheme coalesced into a single, powerful desire: to go home.

He wanted to discuss the ethical implications of host relocation with Oma, but he lacked the nerve to confront him directly. Instead, he found himself achingly nostalgic for his lovely house in Portrush. He missed the simple, unpredictable nature of life on Earth. He didn't like the constant surveillance, the rationed freedom, the pressure of the missions. He needed to find out if there was a way back.

He decided to ask Troy. The AI's response was startling in its clarity. "Rob, the technology exists. Your memory of us, of Beat-a, can be neurologically removed. You can be reinserted into your original time and place on Earth."

"And what about me being a missing person? I have been gone for weeks."

"The authorities can be managed. A story can be fabricated for your absence. It is within our capabilities."

The offer was everything he thought he wanted. "I want normality again," he said, more to himself than to Troy.

He called Oma and explained how he felt. "I thought you liked it here," Oma said, a note of genuine surprise in his voice.

"I do," Rob admitted. "Parts of it are amazing. But I feel a big part of me, a fundamental part, misses home. I cannot ignore it."

Oma was silent for a moment. "I will call in personally in half an hour."

True to his word, Oma arrived at the apartment. His demeanor was serious but not unkind. "Is this really what you want, Robert?"

"Yes," Rob said, his voice firm. "It is."

"Ok. We can do this for you. The process involves a neuralizer to remove the specific memories of your time with us. You have been missing for six weeks on Earth, but we can use time travel to reinsert you at a point just after you left. It will be as if you never disappeared. You will have no knowledge of us, of the Lavas, of any of this."

"And my money? The lottery win?"

"All those memories will remain intact. Your bank account will be untouched. We can make it a smooth transition."

A wave of relief washed over him. "Please, can I go back then?"

"Yes," Oma said. "And do not worry about the two jobs scheduled for Saturday. I will handle them. You can go back tomorrow."

"Ok, Oma. Thank you. I have had a great time and experienced some truly amazing things."

Oma nodded.

"There is one condition. We cannot remove the neural chip. It is a safety precaution. If anything goes wrong for you on Earth, if you are in mortal danger, the chip will allow us to extract you. You are still a part of us, Robert. If that happens, we can restore your memory and give you your life back here."

The terms were accepted. The procedure was carried out. Rob returned to Earth with his mind wiped clean of the previous six weeks, the memory of Lama and the Lava completely erased.

CHAPTER NINETEEN
ECHOES OF A FORGOTTEN LIFE

Two months passed. Rob Reid's mind was happy, untroubled by the memories that had been surgically removed. He settled back into his life in Portrush with ease, training in his home gym, eating well, and enjoying the comforting rhythm of a normal existence. He had been to Belfast many times and had not bumped into that man, Michael, the one he would have remembered as a "crazy guy." Yet, a faint, curious itch remained in the back of his mind about how that stranger had known him.

It was a Wednesday. He had a dental check-up scheduled in Belfast for 11 AM the next day. He felt a bit of pain in his wisdom tooth and was concerned it might be bad.

That afternoon, he went into Portrush for lunch at a place near the train station he frequented, not fancying cooking for himself. He ordered a steak and kidney pie with vegetables and champ, washing it down with a Coke. After lunch, he took a walk along the coast. The weather was typically brisk, with a wind carrying a light rain. He did not stay out long, as he was not wearing a coat. The town was quiet, filled with shops selling holiday trinkets, rock candy, and honeycomb to tourists.

Later, while driving back home, he received a call from Paddy. He had forgotten about their golf game scheduled for

Thursday. He mentioned the dentist appointment, and Paddy chuckled, saying, "It will save you a fiver."

Thursday morning was cloudy and windy. He had a leisurely breakfast before heading down to Belfast for his 11 AM appointment. The check-up revealed he needed a filling, which was scheduled for the following Monday.

Afterward, he decided to walk around Belfast, window shopping. His mind was idle, thinking of little more than his slight toothache. Then, something impossible happened. A voice, clear and distinct, but not his own, spoke in his mind.

Michael, how are you? And how is Lori?

Another voice, familiar yet alien, responded. We are both fine, Lama. How is Rob?

He has been to the dentist. He is a bit grumpy.

Rob stopped dead in the middle of the sidewalk. "What the hell?" he whispered aloud, his heart beginning to race. "I am cracking up."

Without conscious thought, his mind formulated a question aimed at the voice. Lama? Where are you?

The response was immediate and clear. Castle Court.

CHAPTER TWENTY
THE REAWAKENING

Rob stood frozen on the street, a cold dread and a terrifying familiarity warring within him. The voice in his head was not his own, yet it felt like a part of him that had been sleeping had suddenly jolted awake. The name "Lama" echoed with a significance he could not place but could not ignore.

He found his feet moving, carrying him not toward his car, but back in the direction of the Castle Court shopping center. It was a compulsion, a magnetic pull he lacked the will to resist. His rational mind screamed that this was insanity, a psychotic break, but the voice felt more real than the pavement beneath his feet.

He wandered through the crowds, past shops and food vendors, his eyes scanning faces without knowing what he was looking for. Then he saw them: a man and a woman sitting at a small table in a café area. The man was Michael. He looked healthy, calm, and prosperous, a world away from the desperate figure in the East Belfast bedsit. He looked up, and his eyes met Rob's. There was no surprise in his gaze, only gentle recognition.

Simultaneously, Rob felt a wave of warmth rising from within, a sensation of coming home that was both comforting and horrifying. It was Lama. The Lava had been dormant, subdued by the control implant, but it had never truly been erased. The chip Oma had left as a safeguard had somehow acted as a conduit, and proximity to another host had reestablished the connection.

Michael gave a slight, almost imperceptible nod. No words were spoken aloud, but a message was transmitted, a data packet of restored memory flooding Rob's mind.

He saw everything. The multi-story car park. Oma. The lottery. The missions. The trip to 1985. Beat-a. The final choice. It all returned in a dizzying and overwhelming cascade. He remembered the warmth of the eternal sun on Beta-2, the sound of the grandstand at St Andrews, and the desperate face of the woman in Donaghadee.

He stumbled back, leaning against a wall for support. He was not going insane. The past six weeks had been real. They had been erased, but they were real. And he was still a host. Lama was still with him.

The voice in his head spoke again, gentle now. We are here, Rob. We never left. The door back is always open.

He saw Michael and his companion stand up and walk away, melting into the crowd without a backward glance. They had delivered their message, triggered the reawakening.

Rob finally made it to his car, his hands shaking as he gripped the steering wheel. He did not drive home immediately. He sat there, in the dim light of the parking garage, and wept. He wept for the normal life that had been a beautiful, fragile illusion. He wept for the loss of a forgetfulness he now realised he cherished. He wept from the sheer, terrifying wonder of it all.

He was not just Rob Reid, lottery winner from Portrush. He was Robert Reid, operative for an advanced interstellar species, host to a Lava named Lama, and a man who belonged to two worlds, whether he liked it or not. The choice he had made was unmade. His story was not over. It had only just begun again.

CHAPTER TWENTY-ONE
THE REUNION AND THE REVELATION

Rob stood frozen in the middle of Castle Court, the cacophony of the shopping center fading into a dull hum. The voice in his head was not a hallucination; it was a conversation. He was hearing the internal communication between Michael, his Lava Lori, and his own dormant Lava, Lama. It was a channel that had been switched back on.

"Michael appeared.' Not you again,'" Rob muttered to himself, repeating the words he'd just heard internally.

Hi Lama. Hi Lori. Hi Michael, his own thoughts responded, as if on autopilot.

"You really don't know us," Michael said aloud now, approaching him with a look of concern. "There's a Lava inside you called Lama. You're a host. That's why you earned that lottery win. Lama chatted to me; I could hear it talk. Lori, my Lava, talks to me too."

Rob, too bewildered to protest, allowed Michael to steer him to a small cafe. "Come for a coffee. You had a coffee? Get another one."

Over a second cup, Michael explained his new life. "Lori tells me which teams to bet on. I win small bets every week on football teams. Sometimes three hundred dollars, sometimes more. I also get benefits because of my mental health status. It's a good life."

He leaned closer, his voice dropping. "You were part of a team that saved suicides from death and used us as hosts. They watch us to see if we are behaving correctly. They must have cleared your memory of all this and then sent you back."

Rob could only utter a single word. "Wow."

Just then, Oma walked around the corner and sat down at their table without invitation. "It is all true, Robert. You work for us. We wiped your memory and sent you back in time to resume your life."

Oma proceeded to explain everything, confirming Michael's story. Then his tone grew grave. "We are in a predicament. We need you back and operational. The Temporal Transit Authority has discovered our operations. One of our hosts talked. The host's Lava managed to send a warning message indicating that the T.T.A. is setting up fake suicides, both mental health cases and ordinary ones, to stop or capture us."

"T.T.A.? What is that?" Rob asked, the acronym feeling strangely familiar on his tongue.

"Time Travel Awareness," Oma stated. "This is a real and present danger. We need you to come with us. We need to restore your memories."

As if on cue, two large operatives arrived. They did not speak, merely gesturing for Rob to follow. He was led through a shimmering, open passage of light that materialized between two shopfronts, unnoticed by the passing shoppers. They emerged into a sterile, brightly lit laboratory.

The process of memory restoration was not painful, but it was profoundly disorienting. It was like watching the fastest, most intense film of his life, but he was the protagonist. Every mission, every trip, every conversation with Oma and Lama flooded back into his consciousness. He was suddenly, acutely aware of the entire operation.

Oma was waiting when the procedure was complete. "We have a significant problem, Robert. One that might end our operations entirely. The T.T.A. is submitting false death reports of suicides. When we go back to recruit, they are waiting for us in a tactical ambush. We are in serious trouble."

CHAPTER TWENTY-TWO
A NEW STRATEGY AND A STARK WARNING

The revelation meant that early extraction for all known hosts was a strong possibility. It was only a matter of time before Earth authorities, guided by the T.T.A., began systematically questioning mental health patients to see if they had been contacted. The completion of the sister planet's first phase in two months could not come soon enough. Its capacity to house one hundred thousand people would be a monumental help. A directive was sent to all hosts: if questioned, they were to say nothing. Their Lavas would help monitor their emotional state and compliance.

Rob returned to his room after the intense briefing. The familiar environment was a comfort. "Troy, buddy, you are still here."

"Of course, I am your assigned unit. Do you require food?" the AI asked in its firm, pleasant manner.

"Yes, a takeaway. Can you order a three-piece meal from Funky Chicken and a Coke?"

"No problem."

The "time boys," as Rob now thought of the operatives, had been meticulous. They had returned him to the day before he had left, so his absence would not be noticed. Yet, his head throbbed with the re-integrated memories, a phantom pain from a forgotten life.

He ate his chicken and retired for an early night, exhausted by the sheer volume of information he had to process. He woke to peace. Troy was cleaning the bathroom. Rob had eggs and a protein shake, and then spent an hour in the gym, trying to ground himself in physical routine.

Be careful from now on, Lama communicated, its presence now a welcome familiarity. Things are changing. If they catch you, you must hit the panic button. It will bring you home. Well, to here. You have two homes now.

A knock at the door interrupted his thoughts. It was Tam. "Good to see you, Rob."

"You too, Tam."

"You have a meeting in the seminar room in ten minutes."

"Ok."

In the seminar room, Oma spoke first. "Well, it did not work out, your return to your home world. Too many hosts there know you."

"Yeah, you were correct there," Rob admitted.

"I hope you will see this world in a new light now."

"Yes, Oma."

The head of the council cleared his throat, commanding attention. "We have a significant amount to cover. Off world, recruitment of hosts is suspended indefinitely due to these fake suicides designed to trap us. We are noticing alarmingly high numbers in suicide reports, clearly intended to tempt us into a response. Police files on suicides are elevated. The situation looks extremely dangerous."

CHAPTER TWENTY-THREE
THE CHESS GAME

A new, precarious reality set in. "We are aware now that they are aware of us," the council head stated at the next briefing. "But they now know that we are aware of them. It is a stalemate built on mutual intelligence."

The strategy was adjusted. "There are seven suicides reported this week. The reports come in two days after the deaths. We will pick the ones that look the easiest, the most legitimate. If we are trapped, we hit the panic button immediately. That protocol is clear. The next rule is this: if the host does not seem right, if the situation does not feel like a genuine suicide, you walk away. Do not engage."

The council head paused, letting the gravity of the situation sink in. "We believe their ultimate goal is to steal our technology. Any military organization would covet the power to go back and change historical events. For this reason, we have undertaken a contingency plan. We have downloaded as much information as we can on each year of human history from our records. This archive will serve as a baseline."

He explained the implications. "If they successfully steal a device and change history, a dedicated team will be dispatched to locate the change, fix it, or catch the perpetrators in the act and retrieve the technology." He cleared his throat. "Thank you for your patience. You are dismissed."

As everyone filed out, Oma placed a hand on Rob's shoulder. "Do not worry. We will not let them catch us."

The reassurance was short-lived. That evening, Oma came to Rob's room in an agitated state. "Are you ok?" Rob asked.

"No," Oma replied. "A team in America attempted to go back one full day to collect a host. It was a fake. The team was apprehended by a group of military-trained forces. Our operatives managed to get away using the panic button, but they were forced to leave the time device behind. The T.T.A. has finally caught us out. They have our technology."

The response from the superiors was unexpectedly calm. "They wish to observe their progress. We are to do nothing for now. This will be a study of human awareness and reaction to new technology. We will watch their next move. Time travel might help them if they use it wisely.

"

CHAPTER TWENTY-FOUR
A CHANGED WORLD AND A
CONTEMPLATED ALLIANCE

All off-world operations remained suspended. Two months passed. Initially, every year in the historical record remained as it was. The first phase of the sister planet, Beta-a 2, was completed and ready for occupancy, with a capacity for one hundred thousand. However, they had only managed to extract ten thousand hosts from Earth before the operation was noticed. Local news channels began reporting on the mysterious disappearances.

Fifty thousand residents from an overpopulated sector of Beat-a were relocated to Beta-a 2, leaving room for forty thousand more. The mass relocation of three thousand people from Belfast was impossible to hide. The official explanation, when one was desperately sought, was attributed to aliens. "Probably right, I suppose they are," Rob mused when he heard the reports.

Then, the changes began. They were subtle at first. The military, now in possession of the time technology, started to make alterations. They stopped the atom bomb. The device was never detonated; thousands of lives were saved instantly. The council on Beat-a monitored the historical ripple and, after much debate, let the change stand. It was, they concluded, a destructive weapon whose elimination benefited humanity.

A period of quiet followed. Then mobile phones were invented ten years earlier than in the original timeline. The technology arrived prematurely, accelerating human communication. The council was intrigued but not overly worried.

Then came a monumental change. They saved President Kennedy from assassination. The military was definitely working behind this intervention. The ripple effect was more subtle than one might expect, but it was profound. Kennedy served out his term, and his influence altered the course of American politics.

The interventions continued, showcasing a creative and life-preserving intent. They prevented the death of Buddy Holly. The engine of the light aircraft refused to start, and the occupants never took off. Buddy Holly did not die that day. He went on to create more great music, lived to the age of sixty-five, and died of a heart attack, leaving behind two children.

The council on Beat-a studied these changes intently. The pattern was clear: the humans with the technology were not using it for conquest or personal gain. They were using it to heal historical wounds, to save lives, and to foster a better, albeit different, world.

A once-unthinkable idea began to take root. The military's actions demonstrated a responsibility that the council had not believed them capable of. After extensive analysis and debate, the council concluded that humanity, or at least this faction of it, could be trusted. They were no longer just a problem to be managed; they were a potential partner.

The council contemplated a formal alliance.

The contemplation was not idle. It sparked a series of high-level strategy sessions, the details of which were relayed to key operatives, such as Oma and Rob. The vision was no longer merely one of coexistence, but of co-creation.

"The sister planet is the key," the council's spokesman explained to them in a news briefing. "Beta-a 2 is not just a refuge for our overpopulation; it can become a joint venture. A prototype for a society built by both our species. The construction you witnessed, Rob, is only the first phase."

Rob, now fully reinstated and privy to these top-level discussions, listened intently. "A prototype for what?"

"For a new beginning," Oma interjected, a rare spark of excitement in his voice. "The humans have shown a talent for using technology to improve the quality of life. Imagine that ingenuity applied here, without the constraints of Earth's history. The bots work under the eternal daylight, their progress unhindered by night. They don't just build cities; they weave ecosystems. The park you saw is not for ornamentation; it is a functional biome, a life-support system of breathtaking complexity."

The spokesman manipulated a holographic display, showing blueprints of Beta-a 2. "Qualification for relocation is now being re-evaluated. It will not be based solely on operational value. We will seek pioneer hosts and humans who demonstrate adaptability, empathy, and a skill set valuable to a nascent civilization. Engineers, artists, agriculturists, teachers. Your experience, Robert, in bridging both worlds, would make you a prime candidate."

The concept was staggering. It wasn't just an escape; it was an invitation to help build a utopia.

"But an alliance requires trust from both sides," Rob noted. "How do we approach them? After all, we've been abducting their citizens for years, from their perspective."

"Acknowledged," the spokesman said. "The first step is transparency. We will initiate contact with the military faction that possesses the device. We will not demand its return. Instead, we will offer them something they cannot get anywhere else: context."

"Context?"

"We will open our historical archives to them," Oma clarified. "We will show them the full, unvarnished truth of our plight, the slow fading of our race, the desperate rationale behind the Host Accord. We will admit our moral ambiguities. And then, we will show them Beta-a 2. We will propose a treaty: in exchange for their continued responsible stewardship of time travel on Earth, we offer them a seat at the table here. A chance to guide the development of a new world, to ensure its laws and culture reflect the best of both our species. They can select a contingent of their best and brightest to join the first wave of settlers."

The plan was audacious. It was a gamble based on the hope that the humans' demonstrated compassion would extend to a species they had once seen as an adversary.

"The population on Beat-a 2 would be a hybrid," the spokesman continued. "A mixture of relocated hosts from Earth, volunteers from Beat-a, and these new human partners. Their children, born under the eternal sun of a new planet, would be the first true citizens of this alliance. Perhaps some of their daughters would become Queens, not as a secret biological function, but as a celebrated, integral part of a new society's foundation."

Rob looked at the schematics of the soaring, crystalline cities and the vast, green parks. He thought of the constant, reassuring presence of Lama in his mind. A sense of purpose was replacing the fear and confusion he had felt. The road here had been paved with desperation and secrets, but the destination now looked like something out of a dream. The suicide con had begun with a trickle of hope offered to one desperate man on a ledge. It was ending with the potential for a flood of hope for two entire civilizations.

The alliance was no longer just a contemplation; it was a blueprint for survival, and for the first time, it felt like a future worth fighting for.

ABOUT THE AUTHOR